Gum Is Fun!

JENNIFER B. STITH • LISA PERRETT

Carson Dellosa Education®

Bud has gum.

Yum!
PUG

Bud got gum on
the bus.

Fun!
PUG

The gum is on
the rug.

Tug!

Bud got gum
on Pug!

Yuck!
PUG

Gum is on Pug
and Bud!

Run!
PUG

Bud and Pug got in
the tub.

Rub, rub, rub.
PUG

Bud and Pug got a mom hug.

POP!
PUG

Phonics Focus Words: Short u

Bud	Pug	tub
bus	rub	tug
fun	rug	yuck
gum	run	yum
hug		

Decodable Words:

got	mom	pop
in	on	

High-Frequency Words:

a	has	the
and	is	